THE THIEF'S LOVER

COD COVE

BOOK ONE

SADIE KING

THE THIEF'S LOVER

CRIMINAL DESIRES

Mom always told me my sassy mouth would get me into trouble, and I guess she was right. But is trouble meant to feel this thrilling?

A partners in crime, curvy girl romance with a hint of darkness and a whole lot of steam.

I'm a thief. I steal things—beautiful things, shiny things. When Chastity gets in my way, I steal her too.

She's the most beautiful shiny object I've ever possessed.

But this poor little rich girl has a daring streak, and together we're unstoppable. Ransacking the rich. Distributing to the poor.

Until I find out who her father is. He's the most powerful and hated man on the Sunset Coast.

And I've got his most treasured possession…

The Thief's Lover is a wrong-side-of-the-tracks instalove romance featuring an obsessed thief and the curvy girl who steals his heart.

1

WILL

My knife slides down the side of the window frame until I hear the tell-tale click of the lock giving way. Carefully pulling the knife back, I slide my fingers under the frame and jimmy open the window.

Adrenaline pumps through my body, and I throw a glance over my shoulder to the front of the house. There's a low retaining wall that separates the place from the road and, beyond that, the ocean.

My eyes strain in the dark, searching for any sign of movement.

Satisfied that I'm not being watched, I turn back to the window.

Resting my hands on the windowsill, I pull myself up and into the house, dropping down onto a plush carpeted floor.

I stay low, crouched in the unfamiliar corridor, my ears straining for any noise. The only sounds I hear are the waves crashing against the beach from across the road and faint music from the row of bars and restaurants at the far end of the beach.

I watched the owners leave almost an hour ago, dressed up in a fancy suit and chic silk dress. My guess is they've gone to the yacht club, where all the rich folks go for dinner. I'm sure they won't be back for at least another hour, but my blood still thrums in my ears, the excitement I always feel coursing through my veins like a live wire.

Moving quickly and quietly, I creep down the corridor. The first door I try leads to a bedroom.

It has a single bed with plump, fluffy cushions and a poster of some rock band I've never heard of on the wall. The walls are plastered with photos and pictures, and there's pots of nail polish and makeup brushes strewn on the dresser.

For a moment, I'm tempted to rummage through the drawers. There might be a sweet sixteen diamond-encrusted tiara—or whatever the fuck rich people give their daughters—but I resist the urge and close the door.

The best stuff will be in the master bedroom.

I find it at the end of a corridor. This bedroom is as neat as the first one was messy. Plush bedding and an excess of pillows sit neatly on an oversized bed.

Heading to the walk-in closet, I flick on my headlamp. The closet door rolls open, revealing rows of sparkling shoes, designer handbags, and more outfits than anyone could wear in a year.

"And this is only the beach house," I mutter to myself.

It blows my mind the amount of money some people have. They probably come here for only a few weeks out of the year, yet the contents of the closet could feed a family for months.

Ignoring the designer shoes, which are too much of a hassle to shift, I move handbags out the way until I find what I'm looking for. On the last shelf of the closet, tucked away enough so it's not immediately visible, is a red velvet jewelry box.

"Bingo."

Being careful not to knock anything out of place, I pick up the velvet box in my gloved hands. My heart thumps in my ears. I imagine this is what a hunter feels when stalking his prey.

Slowly opening the box, my headlamp illuminates the sparkle of jewelry.

"Gotcha."

There's a gold bracelet with a line of tiny diamonds set in the middle. I hold it up to the light and can't help the grin on my face. It's beautiful. It'll fetch a good price.

Sliding the bracelet into my pocket, I rummage through the jewelry box. There's a set of matching earrings, which go straight into my pocket, and an old-fashioned ring.

I hold the ring up to the light, and the jewels twinkle enticingly at me. It's got two diamond encrusted twists on each side of the square ruby, 1920's style. There are tiny scratches on the band, like it's been well worn, well loved.

It's probably a family heirloom, passed down from a long-dead relative.

I slip the ring back into the box. It would have gotten a good price, but I'm not in the habit of stealing sentimental stuff.

There's a fine gold chain, and I pocket it, too, before returning the box to its place on the shelf. Being careful to put everything back as I found it, I retreat out of the closet.

Depending on how often they get dolled up, it could be weeks before they notice anything is missing.

That's my strategy. Take only what I need. Don't get greedy. Get in, and get out.

I flick my headlamp off and find my way back to the window I came in through.

Hauling myself through the window, I jump silently down to the ground. My eyes and ears strain as I crouch in the grass.

But there's nothing but the quiet road and the beach beyond.

I push the window closed and keep to the shadows as I move down the driveway toward the road.

I'm almost at the retaining wall when a shape moves in the darkness.

I freeze.

There's a woman sitting on the retaining wall. She's hidden in the shadows, which is why I didn't see her before.

As I step closer, she shifts, and her face tilts into a gap where the moonlight is coming through the trees.

My breath hitches in my throat, and I forget to breathe.

She's stunning, with a perfect oval face and long hair waving in the sea breeze. And her figure—cast into shadows by the moonlight, the dips and crevices of her curves could bring a man to his knees. My blood thunders in my ears, and my dick hardens.

The tree moves in the breeze, casting her face back into shadow before I can see the color of her eyes. The eyes that are staring straight at me.

2

CHASTITY

The thief stops dead in front of me, staring like he's never seen a woman before.

Dressed all in black, I barely see him in the shadows, but I hear his breathing. He's surprisingly big for a burglar, yet he's nimble. He jumped from the window, silent and sleek like a cat.

I should feel scared, but all I feel is curious.

He's not carrying a TV, but there's no question he's up to no good. You don't jump from a window unless you're burgling the place.

I tilt my head to the side, regarding him. "Did you get much?"

He takes a step forward, and his hand goes to his belt, where I guess he's got a weapon. A thrill goes through me, which is so wrong, but I've never come face to face with a burglar before.

"I don't know what you mean."

His voice is low and rumbly and sends a delicious thrill down my spine. He sounds casual, and I'd almost believe he was out for an evening stroll if I hadn't just seen him climb through a window.

"I saw you jump out that window."

"Locked my keys outside."

A chuckle escapes my lips. "I've never heard that one before."

I should be scared, but the truth is, I don't care. Having banter with a burglar is the most fun I've had in ages.

He swallows hard and runs a hand over his stubble. It's satisfying to know I've got him rattled.

"I suppose gloves are back in fashion too?" I gesture toward the black gloves he's wearing.

He takes a step closer, and now I can see his eyes. They're dark as the night and fixed intensely on me.

"I suggest you go home, girlie, and forget what you saw."

"Girlie?" Oh, now he's got me angry. "I'm not a girlie."

I slide off the wall to face him. I'm not sure what I'm going to do, but no one calls me girlie.

Especially not someone dressed like they just stepped out of a burglar fashion catalog. No matter how well the sleek black outfit molds to his chest muscles, which I can see better now that he's in a patch of moonlight.

We're breathing hard as we stare each other down.

Suddenly, there's a glint of steel. He moves quickly. There are rough hands on my shoulders, then he's got my arm pinned behind my back.

"Sorry, sweetheart, but you're gonna have to come with me." I struggle against him, feeling a tremor of fear for the first time. "Just for the night. I'll drop you off somewhere tomorrow, but I need to know you're not gonna call the cops."

"I'm not gonna call the cops, asshole."

"Where's your phone?"

"My jacket pocket."

He slides a hand into my pocket and takes my phone, slipping it into his pocket.

"Are you going to kill me?"

"No." His hot breath on my neck makes my hairs stand on end. "I'm gonna steal you."

Oh my. The words send a delicious tremor through my body,

causing a hot sensation between my legs, turning the fear to something else. Something that makes my whole body come alive.

This is much more exciting than college, much more exciting than the boring family lunches and art auctions that my mom organizes.

I should be terrified, but as he leads me to his car and wraps a blindfold around my eyes, it's not terror that I feel but a powerful bolt of excitement.

Mom always told me my sassy mouth would get me into trouble, and I guess she was right. But is trouble meant to feel this thrilling?

3

WILL

My fingers tug on the fabric of the blindfold, testing its resistance. The woman gives an annoyed, "Ow."

It makes her full lips pout in such a way that I have to resist the urge to kiss them.

Don't get distracted.

But I'm already distracted. With her eyes behind the blindfold, I take the opportunity to run my gaze over her plumb body.

Her breasts strain at the seams of a white tank top with a denim jacket over the top. Her style looks casual: denim jacket and leggings. But they're not the kind you pick up from Walmart. The stitching in the jacket is too fine, the fabric too delicate. She may be dressed casually, but it's money casual.

Even her sneakers are a label most girls her age couldn't afford.

Who the hell is she?

It doesn't matter. I've got her in my car now, in the back seat with her hands loosely tied and a blindfold over her eyes.

She's as precious as the jewels in my pocket, and I'm stealing her alongside them.

"Where are you taking me?" she asks as I start the engine.

"Now that would be telling."

"Is it back to the bat cave or something?"

I smile. She's sure got a mouth on her. "Something like that."

It's probably excessive, the blindfold, but I don't want her to see where I'm taking her. If she's a local, she'll figure it out pretty quickly, but I'm hoping to disorientate her.

"What's your name?"

I glance at her in the rearview mirror. Her head turns as she hears my voice.

"Chastity."

"Chastity." I roll the name over on my tongue. It's nice. It suits her.

"What's your name?"

I'm not stupid enough to tell her that. Instead, I keep silent.

She sighs. "I'm not gonna go to the police. Although I should since you are kidnapping me."

"Not kidnapping."

"What would you call this then?"

"I'm stealing you."

This doesn't seem to bother her. In fact, she barely put up a fight when I told her I was taking her. It's almost as if she wanted to go with me.

"What were you doing in Cod Cove, Chastity?"

"I work there."

Even though I can't see her eyes, she turns away as she says the lie. But I don't push.

"How about you? You been a thief long?"

I chuckle. "Not really."

"I can tell."

The comment pulls me up short. "What do you mean?"

"The way you came out of the window. I heard you coming a mile away. You were clumsy, practically fell out of that window."

This is too much; I've worked hard to be good at what I do. "I think I'm pretty nimble for a big guy, actually."

"Nimble? My granny's more nimble than you are. Lucky it's charity night at the yacht club or else all the residents of Cod Cove would have heard you fall."

The laughter bubbles up inside of me before I can stop it. I try to rein it in and be pissed off, but she's too funny. She laughs too, a soft rumble that shows off her generous mouth and high cheek bones.

My jewel has some sass, that's for sure.

I was just going to drop her off farther up the road with no phone, ensuring I was long gone by the time she got back to town. But dammit, I like having her around. Besides, it's not cool to drop a woman off on her own at night. I wasn't thinking straight when I decided to take her. But now I am. And she's coming back to my place.

To disorientate Chastity, I take windy roads and go the wrong way up the coast before doubling back. An hour later, we turn into Temptation Bay, the small beach town where I live. My place is at the end of town, a lonely shack on the edge of the cliff. But there's something I must do first.

We turn down a side street heading away from the beach. There's a run-down trailer park here, and I pull up out front.

Cutting the engine, I turn to Chastity.

"I need to stop in here for five minutes." I eye her warily, wondering if this is the last time I'll see her. "I won't be long. Stay in the car and keep your head down."

It's a risk. If she's going to run, this is where she'll do it. But I need to give her that opportunity. If she wants to go, she can go. There's not a person here who'll say they know me if the cops come looking. I'll have enough time to pack up my belongings and move on.

But I hope to God she doesn't run.

4

CHASTITY

The driver's door slams, and I hear footsteps on gravel. A moment later, the trunk opens, and there's the sound of rustling plastic.

My heart rate quickens. Maybe he's got a body in there, and we've stopped to bury it. I dismiss the thought. Whoever this man is, he doesn't seem the type to have bodies in the trunk.

The footsteps fade away, and all I hear is the thumping of my own heart.

If I'm going to escape, now is the time to do it.

My wrists twist in the restraints, the fabric chafing against my skin. I pull and twist, and slowly, the knot comes loose. My hand slips out easier than it should, leaving me wondering why I didn't try to get out of my restraints earlier.

Pulling the blindfold off, I peer at my surroundings.

We're on the side of a road near a trailer park. There's a cluster of buildings and rusty campers with grass growing around the wheels. It's late at night and quiet, but a few lights shine through the windows.

Throwing the blindfold on the car seat, I push open the door and slip out.

My heart's in my throat as I drop to the ground. Now that I'm free, I'm not sure which way to go, or what I should do. I could knock on any of the trailer doors and report the handsome stranger who kidnapped me, but the truth is, I'm not sure I want to.

He was stealing from people who have far too much money. Is it really a crime?

Keeping crouched over, I make my way between the trailers. As I creep through the park, I hear the rustle of plastic. My body freezes. Then he comes into view. The thief, carrying a bunch of plastic bags.

I tuck myself into the shadow alongside a camper and watch him.

The man crouches outside a trailer and leaves a bag on the doorstep. What is he, some kind of drug courier doing home delivery?

He moves around the corner, and I sneak across the path to the bag he just left. Slowly parting the plastic so it doesn't rattle, I peer inside, bracing myself for what I'm going to find.

There's a tin of coffee, a few cans of food, and some plain cookies.

He's delivering food.

I sneak to the next trailer; this one's got a light on, and there's the sound of a baby crying. Peering into the bag, there's coffee, pasta, and diapers.

I sit back on my haunches. The guy's delivering care packages.

Movement catches my eyes across the park. A woman sits in a rocking chair out front of a trailer, the glow of a cigarette in her mouth.

I scurry behind the trailer hoping she didn't see me.

"How's it going, Sue?"

I've only known him for about an hour, but I'd recognize that deep voice anywhere.

"Not too good, Will."

Aha, so that's his name. Will.

He crouches next to the woman and tucks a bag of food under her chair.

"Bless you, you're a saint." She takes a drag on her cigarette. Her face is lined and drawn. It's hard to see in the dim light, but she must be pushing sixty.

"You should be in bed, Sue. It's late." There's a chiding tone to his voice, like he's looking out for her, making me wonder if she's his mom.

"Can't sleep, and besides, I wouldn't want to miss my gentleman caller."

She smiles up at him and bats her eyes. I stifle a smile at this older lady flirting with Will. Not his mom then.

Will sits next to her on a chair.

"Can't stay too long tonight, Sue. I've got someone waiting for me."

My ears perk up at that. Is he talking about me?

The old lady's face lights up. "Is it a young lady?"

He chuckles. "Nah, nothing like that."

Sue's disappointment almost matches my own, and I have to tell myself I'm being ridiculous.

"That's too bad, Will. It's time you found someone nice."

He scratches his stubble, which I'm already picking up is something he does often. "But I've got you, Sue. You're all I need."

She laughs, a low cackle that lights up her whole face.

"Tell me what's been going on. Is the baby walking yet?" he asks.

They lean their heads together and start gossiping about what I assume are the other residents of the trailer park.

I sink back onto my knees.

The guy's a regular Robin Hood. Stealing from the rich to give to the poor.

There's a fluttery feeling in my gut and an awareness of excitement building. I could run, go home to my parents, and keep living the privileged life that I have been, or I could go back to the car and see what happens if I spend a few days with Will.

Watching him talk to Sue—a good-natured grin on his face and a pack of food tucked under the chair—it's not a hard decision to make.

Slinking back to the car, I pull open the door. I've just got my blindfold back on when I hear the driver's door open.

"Hey, beautiful." Oh, I like how that sounds. "Glad to see you're still with me."

"Not really anywhere I could go tied up and blindfolded."

I hear him chuckle. It's a faint, low rumble of a sound that gets my whole body trembling.

He starts the engine. "By the way, your blindfold's upside down."

5

WILL

My nostrils twitch as I'm pulled into consciousness. The smell of frying bacon makes my belly rumble, and I sit up quickly, banging my head on the shelf above the couch. "Ow."

"Morning."

Through blurry eyes, I try to make sense of the scene in my kitchen. Chastity has a smile plastered on her face, and she's standing in front of the stove, a frying pan sizzling behind her. "Are you making breakfast?"

It's a stupid question, but I just woke up and can't understand how the woman I kidnapped last night and brought back to my place is humming to herself while cooking breakfast.

"I found the food in your pantry. I hope you don't mind." She turns to check on the bacon, and the oversized shirt of mine she's wearing rides up her thighs.

That is a sight I could get used to. "Nope. Don't mind at all."

When we got back last night, Chastity was somewhat subdued. I figured if she didn't run at the caravan park, she wasn't going to run now.

I gave her my bed to sleep in, and I took the couch. It's a small one-bedroom wooden shack with the lounge and kitchen in the same room. Perfect for one; crowded with two.

There's a small table and two chairs by the kitchen, and she sets two plates down. "Breakfast is ready."

My gaze doesn't leave her as I sit at the table. When I first saw Chastity last night, she seemed to sparkle; in the daylight with a smile on her face, she's absolutely dazzling.

"Did you sleep okay?"

"Mmm." She swallows her mouthful. "The sound of the ocean always helps me sleep." I know what she means. I'm halfway up a cliff here, and the waves breaking below lull me to sleep at night.

"You got another job today?" She asks it casually, but my body tenses. I still don't know much about this woman. She could be getting more intel before she goes to the cops.

"I'm not going to talk about that with you."

The expression on her face doesn't change. "That's a shame. I have information you might find useful."

She picks up the salt and twists a generous helping onto her eggs. She's acting casual, knowing that she's got my interest. But I'm not going to show her that.

I push some eggs and bacon onto my fork. "And what might that be?"

She takes her time, taking another mouthful and eyeing me as she chews. "Mmm, are these eggs local?"

I finish my mouthful. She wants to play casual; I can do that all day. "One of the locals has chickens. I get them directly from the source."

"They're good."

Her eyes are sparkling with mischief, and I put my folk down, unable to stand it any longer. "Alright, quit playing around and tell me what you know."

She swallows her food, a look of triumph on her face. "So, you are interested."

Interested in her, that's for sure.

"I know house number seventy-two has the maid bring all the luggage up on Thursday night, ready for the lady of the house to arrive on Friday morning."

Now she's got my attention. If the jewels are in town but the house is empty, it's the perfect opportunity for a hit. "No one's in the house on Thursday night?"

"Only the maid whose room is in the basement."

"Nah"—I shake my head—"I only do empty houses. Too risky."

"Come on. You're not afraid of getting caught, are you?"

It's not that. I'm not in this to get as much as I can. I also want to cause as little grief as possible. That's why I have rules: nothing that looks sentimental, and nothing that could lead to any harm or trauma for anyone.

"People are a liability. You don't know who might pull a weapon, or who might get triggered and end up traumatized."

She cocks her head, regarding me, and I notice that her eyes are blue—deep blue, like the ocean. "You're an ethical thief, aren't you?"

I've never heard it put like that before.

She smiles at me. "Stealing from the rich, giving to the poor…"

So, she did see what I was doing last night. I thought I saw her sneaking in the shadows of the trailer park.

"What if I told you the maid was half-deaf?"

That does change things. I sit back, locking my hands together, thinking of the likelihood of a deaf maid hearing me break into a house.

Chastity smiles. I can tell she's excited. She leans forward. "The maid would never know you were in the house. It's the perfect burglary."

She claps her hands together, her eyes flashing in excitement.

Suddenly, I feel a flash of anger.

She has no idea what it's like to grow up in a single-parent household, going to school with a gnawing hunger in your belly and watching other kids throw food away when you haven't eaten anything but butter on toast for three days.

Or hearing other kids talk about their future, when you know you have no prospects and that the future for you is some dead-end job that doesn't pay enough to feed a family.

I push the chair away from the table and stand up, grabbing her wrist. It's like a bolt of heat between us, and her mouth pops open in a perfect pouty O.

"I do what I do because it's the only way I know how to survive."

Her pulse flickers under my wrist, and my heart thumps in time. But I don't let her go.

"This isn't a game, Chastity. If you want games, you should leave. It was a mistake to bring you here."

I drop her wrist, and she rubs the place where I grabbed her. Her expression looks hurt, and I hate myself for doing that to her.

Flushed with anger, I grab my coat and head out the door. It was a mistake to think a woman like her would understand, would fit into my world.

I take the stairs down the cliff two at a time. The waves crashing against the rocks match the thumping of my heart.

I'm angry at myself for bringing her here. It was a moment of weakness. I saw something I wanted. And I took it.

I got greedy, and that's always the thief's downfall.

There's a path at the bottom of the cliff, and I turn toward town. Walking quickly, I get past the rocky cliffs and to the shelter of the marina.

There's a man hosing down the prow of a slick white yacht, one of the tourist boats that has come in for a few days. The passengers are disembarking to explore the local area.

"Morning, Will."

I raise a hand to wave at Freddy, the marine steward.

"You come to look at your girl? A few more payments and she's all yours."

"Thanks, man."

He unlocks the gate, and I stroll down the jetty until I come to the weatherworn yacht at the end. The paint's cracking, and the sail needs repairing. She's a classic '80s design, which is why she's sat here for so long waiting for a buyer.

The moment Freddy told me about the yacht, I knew she'd be mine. But raising the funds to buy her and fix her up is taking longer than I expected, especially since the closure of the packing warehouses along the coast left a bunch of locals out of a job and unable to feed their families.

Half of the cash I make goes to helping others. The rest goes to payments to Freddy.

I just need a few more decent hits and she'll be mine. It'll take a bit more to get her into shape, but then I'll be ready to set off on my one-man trip around the Americas.

Away from this place. Away from the unfairness of small coastal towns struggling to survive next to overblown billionaire towns, which might contain the residents' third or fourth homes.

The paint cracks under my hand as I run it over her prow. The soft sound of the ocean laps against the wood, calming my heart and stilling my mind.

I look out to the vast ocean—nothing but water between here and Australia.

But something's nagging at me, disrupting my calm. Chastity. Thoughts of her pouty lips and sassy mouth fill my mind. Her thighs in my kitchen. The way her mouth turns up into an easy smile.

I reacted out of anger earlier, annoyed by her privileged excitement, upset by the fact that this is all a game to her.

But if she has inside knowledge, I could use that for a few easy jobs to get the cash I need. It might get me out of this hellhole that much quicker.

6

CHASTITY

The cupboard closes as I put the last of the clean dishes away.

Will's been gone for over an hour, and I've spent every minute of it agonizing over whether I should stay or go.

He got angry at me earlier, and I get that. I'm not taking getting kidnapped very seriously because he's right. It is like a game to me. It's the most exciting game I've played in my life, and I don't want it to end.

Ever since he drew a knife on me and ordered me into his car, I've had this unreal feeling like I'm in a movie or something. I'm not scared of him. I've known enough bad guys in my life to know Will isn't one of them.

He's a good man at heart. He wouldn't hurt me, of that I feel sure. Although this is a chance to find out a bit more about him.

Will's hidden my phone away somewhere, and I don't even want to try to guess where the jewelry is hidden. I'm not going to earn his trust if I go poking around. So, I keep my exploration to the items on display in his run-down shack.

There's a shelf in the lounge with a few books on it, and my fingers run over the spines as I read the titles.

Coastlines of South America
Lonely Planet: Peru
And a Spanish dictionary. He's either well-traveled or planning a trip.

I pull out the Peruvian travel guide and flick through the pages.

Smiling locals in colorful festive costumes stare out at me. Another page has ancient remains and overgrown mountain trails, dusty roads, colorful markets, and street food vendors.

A feeling starts in my gut, a pull towards this place. I've traveled with my family, but only ever staying in the best hotels, places where you never have to leave the resort unless it's for a helicopter ride to see the views.

I wonder what it would be like to go wander around somewhere new, trying the street food and chatting with the locals.

The door opens, and relief floods me as Will comes in. Relief that I see reflected on his face.

"You're still here."

"Where would I go?"

I stand up, letting the book fall on the couch. "I'm sorry if I angered you—"

He cuts me off. "I overreacted. I'm sorry."

He takes a step toward me, his chocolate brown eyes staring intensely into mine. He smells like the ocean, fresh and salty. For a moment, I think he's going to kiss me, and we stand awkwardly, looking at each other.

My heart hammers in my ears. He came back, and he's glad I'm still here. He wants me here. My chest swells, and my pulse quickens as his eyes rake over me.

"So, the maid is half-deaf?"

My chest deflates. He came back for the intel. Of course he did. It's got nothing to do with me.

"Yeah." I sit at the table, hiding my disappointment. Stupid disappointment. The guy tied me up and kidnapped me, and I'm disappointed that he's not into me. I need to get a grip.

"The maid at house number seventy-two is half-deaf."

He leans back with his hands behind his head, considering the information.

"She'll be sleeping in the house on Thursday night," I continue. "But her room is in the basement, and the jewelry is on the first floor."

There's a glint in his eye as he watches me, and I can tell he's getting excited. "They have any pets? Any dogs?"

"Only a small chihuahua that the woman carries in her purse."

He rubs his stubble, thinking about it, his look faraway. I want to get his eyes back on me. I want his attention.

"And the house next door, number sixty-eight." Will turns his gaze back to me, and I feel heat in my cheeks. "He's got a mistress, keeps her in an apartment on the hill."

Will frowns. "I don't do apartments."

I lean in, my chest fluttering with excitement. "He gives her expensive jewelry, but he wouldn't dare keep it in the house. There's a gym room in the back of the garden that he's always working out in."

Will leans into me, excitement flickering in his eyes. "Let me guess. That's where he keeps the jewelry for the mistress?"

I smile, and he returns it. "It's got to be. Mrs. Anders would never allow it in the house."

I realize my mistake, and my body goes cold. Will sits back, narrowing his eyes at me.

"How do you know what Mrs. Anders would allow? How do you know all this?"

He's onto me, but I try to keep my expression cool. "I used to work as a cleaner around Cod Cove."

It's a lie, and I make myself hold his gaze as I say it.

Will studies me with his intense look.

I'm not sure he's buying it, but he doesn't push. Maybe it's good enough that I'm giving him the intel. Maybe he doesn't care who I really am.

The thought leaves a bitter taste in my mouth that I can't get rid of. Since when did I care so much about what Will thinks?

I've got an opportunity here to take down the community I hate, to get back at all those privileged, dishonest folk. Like my family. Like me. The thought makes me shift uncomfortably. I'm exactly what Will hates in this world.

But for now, that doesn't matter. We need each other, and this is the best adventure I've had in my life.

"So, which do you want to hit first? Deaf maid or unfaithful husband?"

Will leans forward with a gleam in his eye and a smile turning up his lips.

"Deaf maid first, then the straying husband."

"I'm coming with you."

The words are out before I can think too much about them. Will shakes his head slowly. "Oh no you don't. I work alone."

I wave my hand dismissively, the way I've seen my mom do, as if the matter's already decided.

"I'm coming."

I stick my chin out and meet his gaze. His eyes blaze into mine with a look so intense I feel a shiver all the way through my body.

"I know where the rooms are. I've been inside these houses."

"You really want to become a thief?"

He's regarding me curiously, but the words stir something in me, something that makes my insides flutter. And I don't know if it's him or the daring deeds I'm committing myself to.

"Definitely."

He shakes his head slowly, but he's got a smile on his face. "Okay, Chastity. But you do exactly as I say, all right? No sassing me when we're on a job."

I let out a squeal and jump up from the table. My arms go

around him, and I'm sitting on his lap before I realize what I'm doing.

He feels sturdy under me. Safe and strong.

"Okay, calm down." His mouth is inches from mine, and we stare at each other, both breathing hard. I part my lips, ready for the kiss that I'm sure will come. But it doesn't.

His fingers run over my cheek, and he tucks a strand of hair behind my ear.

"We need to get you something black to wear."

Feeling foolish, I turn away. I practically threw myself at Will, and he didn't do anything.

He's more interested in his jewels than me, I remind myself. I'm only here because I can get him into the houses. I have to remember not to be such an idiot next time.

7

WILL

"Don't hog the binoculars." Chastity pulls at the strap around my neck, and I lower the binoculars and hand them to her.

She's a demanding assistant, but I like having her around, especially now when we're lying on our bellies with our sides touching in the long grass. She's so close I can smell her cherry lip balm and the fresh scent of soap.

An insect buzzes by her hair, and I sweep it away with my hand, taking the opportunity to brush the back of her neck.

"Bee," I say when she gives me a funny look.

I'm not sure if I've gone crazy having Chastity along, but I like her company, not to mention her quick tongue and her body pressed against mine in the grass.

Suddenly, she stiffens, and I draw my gaze from her legs stretched out in the grass to the road below. There's a black car moving along it.

"That's her."

I grab the binoculars off Chastity and focus on the car pulling up to house number seventy-two. "The maid drives a Tesla?"

"It's not hers. It belongs to the family."

I focus the lens on the car as the driver's door opens. A middle-aged woman with long dark hair steps out. She's wearing a pair of black slacks and a neat green blouse. She's not what I was expecting a maid to look like.

"You sure that's the maid?"

The binoculars are around my neck, and Chastity pulls the lenses toward her, bringing our faces close together. She peers through the lens while I watch her plump mouth, only inches from mine.

"Yeah. That's her. What did you expect? Someone in uniform?"

Well, yeah, I did. Just goes to show how much I know about the uber rich. Even the maids dress better than most people.

Taking the lenses back, I watch the woman pull out a key and unlock the house. After a while, she comes back for the bags.

The trunk is packed with suitcases and bags of groceries. "How long they staying for?"

"Probably just the weekend."

I lower the binoculars and peer at Chastity. She seems to know far too much about the people who live in house number seventy-two. For the hundredth time, I wonder who the hell she really is.

"Ooh, is that a PlayStation? Jack must be coming up."

A pang of jealousy stabs at my chest. "Who's Jack?"

Her focus stays down the lens. "He's their son. About the same age as me…"

She's about to say something else but stops herself. "I think," she adds, giving me the lenses back.

I can't hide the scowl on my face. It's not like me to be jealous, but where Chastity's concerned, I can't help myself.

"So how are we going to get in?" she asks, completely unaware of the effect she's having on me.

I swallow the jealous feelings down and try to concentrate on the task at hand. Putting the binoculars back to my eyes, I drag them slowly over the house.

Every place has a weakness, somewhere the cameras can't see, especially up here where the old wooden villas sit on property that's open to the ocean. It supposedly adds to the community feel. Not a lot of big fences or guard dogs here.

I pause as I spy a possible point of entry. "That balcony. On the first floor."

Chastity takes the binoculars and looks where I'm pointing. There's an enclosed courtyard with a wall running around it.

"We can reach the balcony via the wall." She smiles as she sees what I'm suggesting.

"I'll be able to open those French doors, and we'll be in."

"That leads straight to the master bedroom."

She's breathing heavily, getting excited by the prospect. My eyes steal a glance at her breasts heaving up and down, and my dick twitches in my pants. I know exactly what she's feeling because I feel it too: the excitement of planning a hit. But this time it's more intense because Chastity's by my side.

"Are you sure you want to come with me?"

She turns to face me, a smile dancing over her lips. "Hell yeah."

I cup her chin in my hand, unable to resist. "I need to be able to trust you."

"You can trust me, Will." Her blue eyes look up at mine. They're round and innocent.

"Then you need to tell me the truth, beautiful. Because you're not a fucking cleaner. Tell me exactly who you are, Chastity, and how you know this neighborhood so well."

8

CHASTITY

*W*ill's thumb grazes my chin, sending shocks of heat through my body. This is the moment I tell him the truth, tell him who I am. Except as soon as he learns who my father is, he won't want anything to do with me.

"No more lies, Chastity. If we're going to work together, I need to be able to trust you."

Oh damn. It's time to come clean…sort of.

I take a deep breath and let it out slowly, stalling for time. I can't tell Will the whole truth because he'll stop looking at me so intently and calling me beautiful, but I need to give him something.

"I'm not a cleaner."

He chuckles. "I figured that much out."

"I used to come up here a lot with my friend Trinity." It's not quite a lie, but it's not quite the truth either.

"Her parents own one of the houses along here." This is also true.

"The one you were waiting outside of the first night we met?" Will's eyes bore into mine, and I find myself nodding.

"Yeah." I'm relieved that it's true because I can't lie to him when he's looking at me like that.

"What were you doing here that night?"

I look down to the street below and the ocean beyond. This part is harder to tell, probably because it's the whole truth. But I need Will to trust me, and I suddenly realize that I want to tell him. I want to talk to him about this.

"I dropped out of college."

His brow furrows, and I realize how privileged that sounds. From what I've found out about Will's life, he never had the opportunity to go to college.

"I wasn't smart enough." Half of the truth. "My parents wanted me to do a business degree, but I hate it. I know that must sound privileged, but it's hard when your parents have your life mapped out for you and you never have any choices of your own."

I leave out the fact that the mapped-out life was working for my dad and marrying one of his cronies. I don't tell him that my dad gave the college a healthy donation to ensure my place in the class. I don't tell him that the lessons were too hard, that I didn't enjoy studying, that I kept sitting in lectures surrounded by the smart and the privileged thinking *there must be more to life than this.*

"So, you up and left?"

"I failed my last paper. I was going to get kicked out, so I left." That bit is the truth, and it shames me to say it. "I failed college. I'm a dropout."

I hang my head. My parents don't know I've left yet, and they'll be furious when they find out. I'll have to tell them soon, but I don't want to think about that now. I want to live in the moment for once in my life instead of being primed for a life I don't want.

I feel rough fingers on my chin, and Will tilts my head up. "Hey, there's worse things you can be."

His eyes are dancing. I realize he doesn't care that I dropped out of college, and it makes me feel lighter.

"You could be a thief." His lips turn up in a smile and I laugh because, yeah, compared to dropping out of college, this is going to piss my parents off a whole lot more.

"Why did you come up here?" He's not finished quizzing me yet, and I drop my head again, unable to look at him while I'm telling half-truths.

"I didn't know where to go. I have a lot of good memories here. I thought Trinity would be here and that I could hang with her for a few days before I told my parents. Things were always good here. No drama, just hanging by the beach."

Memories flash into my mind of me and Trinity as little girls running barefoot across the sand when we were young and innocent, not yet old enough to understand how my dad made his money.

"Some of the happiest moments of my life were here."

The memory fades, and I turn back to Will. He's looking at me differently, and I wonder if I've won his trust. Everything I said was almost true. There are just a few things I left out.

"How about you? What's it all for?"

He looks past me, out to the ocean, and a faraway look comes into his eyes. "I'm going sailing."

His expression softens as he talks.

"I've got a yacht I'm buying off a guy I know. It needs fixing up, but when I've got enough money together, I'm going sailing."

"Where to?" I already know the answer.

"Around the Americas, Mexico, Peru—wherever the wind takes me."

He looks wistful, and I imagine for a moment what that would be like. Sailing away with Will, not knowing where we'll be the next day. Exploring distant shores, meeting local people.

"It sounds amazing."

"Yeah." His voice changes, and he lifts the binoculars to his eyes. "I only need a few more good hauls and I'll be off."

9

WILL

Clouds obscure the moon, plunging our surroundings into deep shadow as we crouch in the bushes behind house number seventy-two.

It's 2 a.m., and the only sound is the rhythmic crashing of the waves.

Two weeks ago, I threw a rock at the single streetlight along this stretch of the road, smashing it to bits. I'm annoyed, although not surprised, that the council has already replaced it. There's been a light out by the trailer park for almost six months. It's amazing how quickly the council acts when its wealthy constituents need some repairs.

The light casts a pale golden glow over the street and the front lawn. It's not ideal, but at this time of night, I'm counting on there being no one around.

Chastity crouches beside me, looking hot in her fitted black leggings and top. The black fabric clings to her breasts, showing the outline of her nipples. My gaze keeps going there, making it hard to stay focused on the job at hand.

"Do exactly as I tell you. No talking when we get in there."

Her eyes sparkle in the dim light, and there's an excited edge to her voice. "Got it."

We've been over the plan several times, but I can't help feeling a twinge of unease. This is the first time I've taken someone in with me. If that someone wasn't Chastity, I wouldn't do it. But the way her eyes sparkle, her breathlessness… It lets me know she's as excited about this as I am.

I want to share this with her. I want her to experience the adrenaline rush I do. And I need her to keep lookout. At least, that's what I tell myself.

We've been waiting in the bushes for twenty minutes, and there's no sign of movement. It's time to go.

"You ready?" She nods. "Last chance to back out."

She gives me a wicked smile. "Not a chance."

Keeping low to the ground, we cross the distance to the enclosed wall.

At first glance, it's a sheer wall, but what I saw through the binoculars earlier today were the indents created by the pattern of the wall. With my climbing shoes on, I find a foothold and pull myself up onto the wall.

Once over, I reach a hand down to help pull Chastity up.

Then it's easy to swing ourselves over the glass panel of the balcony and drop to the wood below.

My heart's thumping in my ears as we crouch, listening for signs that anyone heard us.

Satisfied we're alone, I slide the knife from my backpack.

The doors to the balcony are classic French doors, which means it takes some jimmying of the lock before it pops out of place. With a gloved hand, I turn the handle and step into the room.

It smells like stale perfume and musty carpets, like it's been locked up for a while.

Chastity comes in behind me, breathing hard. She's on tiptoe, the excitement making her body quiver. I can't help myself. I place a hand on her back, and she snaps her head around to look at me, her eyes bright with excitement.

My body pulls toward her, the adrenaline setting all my nerve endings on fire. The urge to kiss her is so strong. I lean toward her before remembering where we are and what we're doing.

Snapping my attention back to the job, I give her the signals we agreed upon earlier so we could communicate without talking.

With my finger, I point to her and then the floor, and she crouches obediently, understanding I want her to wait here and stay low.

My eyes adjust to the dark as I take in what appears to be a sitting room. There's a chaise lounge facing the window and a cabinet to the side.

One door leads to the right, and another leads to the left. I'm uncertain which one to take and look to Chastity and her inside knowledge. She shrugs her shoulders. I guess her visits to the neighborhood didn't extend as far as the personal quarters of the lady of the house.

Choosing the door on the right, I push it open gently. It opens without a sound, not surprisingly well oiled.

Behind the door is a small room with a vanity and a full-length mirror. A pink suitcase that I remember seeing the maid unpack earlier stands open by a chest of drawers.

Bingo.

With a quick look back at Chastity, I move through the door and to the suitcase.

It doesn't take long to find the jewelry. There's a thick gold link chain and a set of ruby earrings. I pocket them both as well as a gold bracelet, but I leave behind an antique looking brooch. It's got diamonds encrusted all over it, but the old-fashioned design makes me think it's an heirloom.

I find gold cufflinks that'll melt down to some value and a string of pearls, which I leave. Not much money in pearls.

I mess the suitcase up a bit and set a small ornament on its side. This time, I want it to look like a burglary so the maid doesn't get the blame.

With my pockets stuffed, I move silently back the way I came. It's been less than two minutes, but my haul should bring in enough to keep my community fed for another week, put a decent payment on the boat, and take Chastity out somewhere nice for dinner.

Padding quietly across the floor, I carefully pull the door open.

The French doors have blown open, leaving the curtains billowing into the night, and there's no sign of Chastity.

10

CHASTITY

My blood thunders in my ears, and there's a buzz running through my body that makes me bounce on the balls of my feet as I crouch by the door.

I've never done anything like this in my life. It's thrilling. Part of that is Will. He's so confident and focused and nimble. I never knew burglars could be so damn sexy.

I've been in the Palmers' house hundreds of times, but I've never gone into Mrs. Palmer's room. It's plush, as I'd expect from a woman who carries a dog around in her handbag.

She's my mom's best frenemy. They'll air-kiss when they see each other and ask politely about the children, but then try to outdo each other by seeing who can hold the biggest charity event or whose kid got into an elite college. Oops. My heart clenches at that thought.

My dropping out of college will mean social embarrassment for my mother. I feel a pang of guilt.

But isn't that the reason I dropped out? I have to do what's right for me, even if it means Mrs. Palmer wins gloating rights over my mother for the season.

It's only been a few seconds, but it feels like Will has been gone for ages. He must have found the closet, which means the bedroom is through the other door.

My fingers twitch, and I press my hands together. There might be something in the bedroom that could help my mother get an edge over the Palmers and make up for my drop-out status.

I'm not sure what, though. Maybe the sheets aren't two hundred thread count, or maybe there's a packet of condoms by the bed, which would mean an affair, or an oversized dildo.

Will told me to stay put, but it can't hurt to take a little look. Not when the only other person in the house is peacefully sleeping two floors down.

Padding across the room, I turn the door handle and silently slip into the bedroom.

The curtains in here are closed, and it takes a moment for my eyes to adjust to the dark. There's the outline of a large bed in the middle of the room with cushions piled up on top and a set of drawers on either side.

I move to the first set of drawers, but my eyes haven't fully adjusted and my leg knocks into something hard.

A sharp pain shoots through my shin, and the sound of a thick chair scraping across the wooden floor screeches out.

"Ow."

Now that my eyes have adjusted to the dark, I can see the low chair I walked right into. Something moves in the room, and I freeze.

There's a shape in the bed. What I thought were pillows piled up high is a person.

My heart leaps into my throat, and I stifle a gasp. The shape rolls over in bed as I drop to the floor.

I crawl back to the door as fast as I can, every shuffle ringing loudly in my ears.

My heart's hammering so loud I'm sure the whole street must

hear as I pull open the door and come face to face with an angry Will.

One look at my wide, terrified eyes and his expression changes. I make the sign for *let's get the fuck out of here.*

Although I know he wants to tell me off, we move silently to the French doors and jump off the balcony to the soft grass below.

Will grabs my hand and we run, dodging bushes and leaping over walls, until we get to where we left the car.

I'm confident no one's behind us now, and the cause of adrenaline coursing through my body has changed from fear to laughter.

It bubbles out of me as I pull open the passenger door and dive in.

"What's so funny?" Will asks as he fires up the car. "And what were you doing? You were meant to stay put."

"I heard something," I lie. I can't tell him about wanting to get one over for my mom.

"The maid." I clutch my side laughing. "She was asleep in the bed."

Will concentrates on the road, putting as much distance between us and the house as possible, but his expression softens.

"I thought her room was in the basement?" he says.

"It is." I'm laughing so hard tears are running down my face. "She must sleep in the master bedroom when she knows she's on her own."

Will glances over at me. "That's cheeky of her."

"Cheeky? Mrs. Palmer would have a fit. The maid sleeping on her Egyptian cotton sheets."

Will chuckles. "I take it rich people don't like sharing their beds.'

"Hell no. The maid belongs in the basement, that's what they think. But this maid is giving them her own little fuck you."

Will laughs then as well, and it feels so good, laughing

together. I feel light and free and like I could do anything right now.

Feeling bold, I lean over the space between us and plant a kiss on Will's cheek. At the last minute, he turns his head, catching my lips with his.

11

WILL

Chastity's soft mouth on mine sends zaps of energy coursing through my already electrified body. She tastes like salt and cherry lip balm and everything delicious. But there's something else. The metallic taste of adrenaline coursing through her veins and coming out in her hungry lips.

I should be looking at the road, but I can't tear myself away from Chastity's kiss.

"Watch out!"

She pulls away, and I swerve over to my side of the road. We're on the coastal road with waves crashing on the rocks below, and if we went off the road here, it'd be the end of us.

Chastity giggles, and a thrill goes through me at the sound. I've had a taste of her lips. I've claimed her mouth. Now I can't resist touching her trembling body.

My hand runs up Chastity's thigh, and she shivers underneath my touch.

I steal a glance and see she's turned to face me, her pupils wide. Her teeth rake over her bottom lip as she lays a hand on my thigh.

Her touch is electric, and the bolt that goes through my body makes me forget that I'm driving. All my nerve endings are focused on the heat coming off her touch.

Her hand slides up my thigh. Then she's palming the hard bulge in my pants.

"Careful, honey. That's dangerous."

She snickers, but her hand doesn't stop. "What if I like it a little dangerous?" Her pouty mouth pulls into a mischievous smile.

Holy shit. Her words make my body sizzle. My cock pushes against my trousers, eager to get into her waiting palm.

Her fingers reach for my belt buckle, and I swerve, almost hitting the barrier that leads to the rocks below. I ease my foot off the pedal, slowing down and trying to focus on the dark road in front of me.

"Shit, Chastity. You can't do that when I'm driving."

She giggles as her fingers pull open my belt. "Tell me to stop."

Her hand slides into my pants, and her hot fingers close around my aching cock. "Fuck."

Instead of telling her to stop, I shuffle forward so she can hold all of my shaft.

"You can't do that while I'm driving." My protest sounds feeble even to my own ears.

"Tell me to stop, Will, and I'll stop."

As she says it, she pulls my cock out of my pants and leans over me, her breath tickling the end of my dick.

"Fuck, Chastity, what are you doing?"

She giggles again, and her lips enclose my tip. I let out a groan, and my eyelids flicker shut.

When I open them again, there's a corner coming up, and I have to swerve hard to make the turn.

My heart rate increases. I'm not sure if it's the pressure of her mouth on my cock or the danger of the situation.

"You really can't do this." I pull at her hair, but she only slides her lips open further, taking my length inside her wet mouth.

"Fuuuck."

My body's on fire, and I'm hyped up on adrenaline, though I guess she is too. This is the most exciting, dangerous thing I've ever done. But if we keep this up, I'm going to drive us off the road.

"Honey, I'm gonna have to pull oh-over"

It comes out as a groan as she sucks hard, her mouth moving up my shaft.

There's a pull-off coming up with a lookout area, and I pull into it. The wheels spin as I pull on the hand brake, slamming to a halt right up against the barrier. The ocean crashes below us, but we're shielded somewhat from the road.

My balls are pulled up tight. I could explode right in her mouth, but that's not what I want to do. Taking Chastity gently by the hair, I pull her head back until my cock pops out of her divine mouth.

Her lips meet mine, and I taste my own saltiness on them—and that metallic taste of adrenaline. My hand tangles in Chastity's hair as I kiss her mouth, her neck, her throat. I want to taste every part of her.

She moans as I run my hand over her breasts, pulling her bra down to tug at the nipples I've been aching to touch. But I want to be closer to her. My cock throbs to be inside her.

"Get in the back seat."

We clamber through to the back, and I waste no time peeling off her top and sliding my hand into her bra. Her breasts are milky white and heavy, and I run my mouth over them, sucking on the hard nipples.

The adrenaline makes my movements more urgent, and Chastity matches my urgency. I tug at her leggings and her panties until she's straddling me in nothing but her black bra.

My mouth devours her neck as my hand slides between her legs. She's dripping wet and inviting, ready for me.

My dick's already out, and she guides it to her entrance.

"Wait." I reach into my pocket to get a condom out of my wallet.

She raises an eyebrow. "You carry those around in case you get lucky?"

"I like to be prepared."

I saw my mom struggle as a single parent. There'll be no unplanned pregnancies in my life.

With the condom on, I position Chastity's hips so she's lined up with the end of my cock. Her wide eyes meet mine.

"I've never done this before," she whispers.

"Never made out in the back of a car?"

"Never had sex."

I stop with my dick poised at her entrance. "This is your first time?"

She bites her lip and nods. My heart thumps in my ears. She's a virgin, and I'm going to take her in a quick fuck in the back of a car. This isn't right. Chastity deserves better than that.

"Oh honey, we should be in a bed. Our first time should be special."

She takes my cock in her hand and slides herself onto my tip. "I can't wait for a bed, Will."

Her pussy clenches around my tip, and it takes all my strength not to slam it home. "Honey, are you sure?"

Taking the decision from me, Chastity moves her hips downwards, sliding her pussy a few inches onto my cock.

It's like sliding into paradise. Electric volts shoot through me, making my whole body buzz.

She pulls up quickly with a sharp intake of breath, her face contorting.

"You okay, honey?"

"It hurts."

"You want me to stop?"

"No, keep going. I want all of you."

Grabbing her hips, I thrust upwards. She gasps as my cock

sinks into her. She's tight, her pussy walls squeezing me until I think I'll explode.

We rock for a moment as she adjusts to the new sensation. "I feel so full."

Her tits are pressed against me as I pull her bra off and take one of her nipples in my mouth. "You feel good, beautiful. So good."

She moves her hips back and forth, her eyes widening as she discovers her sensitive spot.

"That's it, honey. Rock against me like that."

She moves back and forth as I lift her hips up and down, the rhythm matching the crashing of the waves far below.

A light shines briefly in the window as a car goes past on the road.

Chastity laughs, and it seems to spur her on.

She's riding me hard, her tits bouncing up and down as she moves against me. There's a sheen of perspiration glistening on her forehead, and the little whimpering sounds she's making let me know she's close.

"Will, I think I'm gonna come."

Her words come out as little moans, and I almost lose it.

"Come for me, baby. Come all over my dick."

"Will!" She cries out as her pussy clenches around me.

The tight convulsions suck the life force out of me until I cum hard into her tight pussy, the pent-up energy of the night building to an explosive release that leaves me shaking as the adrenaline flows out of me.

Chastity collapses on top of me, her hair falling over her bare shoulders, her chest heaving hard.

I kiss her neck, her shoulder, every part of her I can see.

She flicks her hair back, and when her gaze finds mine, she's laughing. "That was wild."

"The sex or the burglary? Or the dangerous driving?"

"All of it."

She's right. Thieving was fun on my own, but with Chastity, it's electrifying. She's intoxicating, turning everything into a game and reminding me how fun life can be.

At first it was a novelty, stealing Chastity away for a while. But as we hold each other in the back seat of the car, with the sound of the ocean far below, I know I want to keep her for good.

CHASTITY

The next few days pass in a happy daze. We spend most of our time in the bedroom. Will can't keep his hands off me, and I don't mind. He explores my body like he loves every curve, and I revel in his attention.

I'm sweating from our morning love making when Will brings me coffee in bed. He's dressed already, which worries me. We've barely put any clothes on for three days.

"You going out?"

He sets the steaming mug on the bedside table. "I need to shift some goods."

I tilt my head, curious. He hasn't told me about this side of the business. "Who's your buyer?"

Will sits on the bed and runs a hand up my bare shoulder, planting a kiss on the spot where it meets my neck. "That's not something you need to worry about."

Will's evasive about this side of the business, and I wonder what he's hiding. "But if we're business partners now, I need to know."

His lips trail down my arm, and a shiver runs through me, making it hard to concentrate. "Who said we were partners?"

I turn around so he can't reach my shoulder and distract me with his lips. "I want to do another job."

His fingers trail up my arm, but I bat them away. "I'm serious, Will. I want in."

He lets his hand fall, finally looking me in the eye.

"There's opportunities out there. We could hit house number sixty-eight, and I haven't even told you about number twenty-two yet."

He cocks his head, listening.

"Which is supposedly empty all summer, but the owner brings his mistress up some weekends. A mistress who always has new and expensive presents from him."

His eyes light up, and I can tell he's interested. "When's the house empty?"

"We'll have to scout it out."

Will looks away, and his hand trails over his stubble. "Isn't your family missing you? Don't you need to go back sometime?"

The last thing I want to do is go back to my family. This is so much more exciting than the life they had mapped out for me. "I've told them I'm staying with a friend."

I messaged my mom when Will gave me my phone back a few days ago.

"They know about college yet?"

I look down. I wasn't brave enough to tell her that bit of news. "Not yet. I'll call my mom soon and tell her."

I don't want to think about my family. I don't want to think about my future. I just want to think about the here and now, with Will, and what I can do to feel that high again that I got after breaking into the Palmers'.

"So how about it? Another job?"

He climbs onto the bed and pushes me gently backward. The sheet falls off my shoulder, exposing my bare breasts and already hard nipples. "I've got a job for you."

I giggle as Will tugs at his belt. "A big job?"

He laughs, and we roll together onto the bed.

As he wraps me in his arms and kisses my neck, I'm filled with happiness and something that I've never felt before: belonging and freedom.

13

WILL

Mine is the only car in a parking lot full of Harleys as I pull up outside The Black Crow. Rock music blares from the juke box as I push open the door and step inside.

There's a group of men sitting at a table, and they all turn to stare at the intruder entering their clubhouse. The black leather jackets with "Underground Crows MC" patched on the back should be enough for any sensible person to back up and leave. But I've never been sensible.

"Will."

One of the men gets up from the table and strides toward me, a smile poking out from behind his shaggy beard.

"Hey, Gage."

I shake his outstretched hand, and he slaps me on the back.

"Let's go up to my office."

I follow Gage up a flight of creaky stairs to the back of the club rooms. He leads me into a small room, and I take a seat opposite him at the table.

"How's business?" he asks.

For my answer, I take the velvet roll out from my pocket and unravel the contents.

The jewelry looks dazzling under the fluorescent lights. The twinkle of gold chains and diamonds and precious stones.

"Business is good."

Gage chuckles and pulls out a jeweler's loupe. He picks up a bracelet studded with diamonds and peers at it through the glass.

"These all real?"

I shrug. "How should I know, man? They came from rich people's houses. I doubt they're fake."

While Gage examines each piece, I sit back with my hands behind my head and wait.

I've been doing business with the Underground Crows for as long as I can remember. For a while, I even considered joining as a prospect.

When you've grown up with just yourself and your mom, struggling to make ends meet, there's a lot of appeal in a motor-cycle club.

But then I got a taste for sailing and the ocean. There's nothing like the calm I feel when I'm out there on the water. I chose water over the road, and I haven't regretted it.

Instead, I sell my wares to the Crows, and they take them across the border, where they're easier to shift to foreign buyers without drawing attention.

I don't get as good a price as if I did it myself, but I'm not greedy. I don't want the hassle of brokering the deal. I like to get the goods out of my hands as quickly as possible in exchange for cash.

Gage sets down his loupe. "I'll give you fifteen grand."

I rub my jaw, considering the offer. The Crows may be my only option for shifting the stuff, but that doesn't mean I can't negotiate.

"This lot is worth at least twenty-five."

The smile has gone from Gage's face, replaced by a hard stare. I match him eye to eye. I'm not afraid of him, and this has always been part of the bargaining. "Twenty."

I take my time, glancing back at the jewels. I already know I'll take his offer, but I don't want to give in too easily.

My gaze rests on a set of earrings—sapphires set in beds of gold. They remind me of the color of Chastity's eyes.

"Twenty." My hand closes over the sapphire earrings. "And I'm keeping these."

The smile returns to Gage's face, and he raises an eyebrow. "Who's the lucky lady?"

"Never you mind."

I hold out my hand, and we shake on the deal.

With my other hand, I pocket the earrings, imagining how they'll look on Chastity's petite ears.

Gage slips an envelope out of his pocket and counts out a wad on hundred-dollar bills. I slip them in my pocket as he rolls up the jewelry.

With our business finished, the easy smile returns to his face. "Come and have a beer."

As we head down to the bar, he hands over the roll of jewelry to another club member and talks low in his ear.

The man heads out the door, and I hear a bike start. I assume they're getting the stolen goods off their property as soon as they can to wherever the hell they keep such things. I don't ask. I don't want to know.

I feel lighter with the twenty grand in my pocket. I'll stop by Freddy's on the way back and put some money down on the boat. Then I'm taking Chastity out to dinner.

14

CHASTITY

Three weeks later...

My fingers trace Beach Head Road on the map spread out on the table. It's the main road through Cod Cove, and red crosses mark off the houses we've hit.

"How about number thirty-four, up the right of way?" asks Will, pointing to a place set off from the main road.

It's where the Fallows live. Mrs. Fallow was always kind to me. I remember her being talked about because she let her hair grow wild and laughed too loud, and she kept the freckles that the sun brought out on her face rather than getting them derma-scrubbed into oblivion at the salon like the other women did.

"They've got Dobermans." It's a lie, but I don't want to steal from Mrs. Fallow.

My finger rests on a street that we haven't touched yet. "How about one of these houses up here?"

I try to remember who owns each of the houses but can't put any faces to them.

Will pulls a different map from underneath and places it on

top. It's a different town farther up the coast. We've be alternating between the towns along the coast, trying to spread out our hits.

The last three weeks have been the most exciting of my life. Every time we hit a place, I get such a thrill, and the adrenaline-fueled sex afterwards is amazing.

Will leans over the map, his breath tickling my ear. "We can take a look. We only need one more good haul and I'll have the yacht paid off."

My chests constricts. Will's got a big grin on his face, and I know the yacht is his dream, but the thought of this all coming to an end makes my chest ache.

When this is over, he sails away into the sunset, and I go back to my family. I pick up my coffee cup and take it to the sink so he doesn't see the expression on my face.

"I've got to make a visit to my buyer today," he says. "I don't like keeping too much stock on site."

By the time I turn back to him, I've composed myself. I hate it that he goes to the buyer alone, like it's a part of the business that I can't be involved in. I want to know everything about how this works.

"I want to come."

He shakes his head. "Sorry, honey. You don't need to be a part of this bit."

His hands slide around my waist, and there's immediate heat between my legs. I know he's trying to distract me. And it's working.

"But what if something happens, and I need to offload the goods?"

"What could possibly happen?" He kisses my neck, making my whole body tremble. I run my hands up his thigh until I'm cupping his bulge in my palm.

"I'll stay in the car. I want to see who you work with." My hands stroke as I say it, and I know he can't think straight while

I'm doing this. "Please, baby. Pretty please."

I whisper the words in his ear, and he moans as I gently squeeze his cock. I've got him in the palm of my hands. Literally.

"All right, all right. Whatever you want, honey."

His arms scoop under my legs, and he lifts me up. "But you're gonna have to earn it."

Will's got a wicked grin on his face as he carries me to the bedroom.

He sets me down on the bed and climbs on top of me, his body pressing me backward.

"I'll earn it."

I get onto my knees and pull at his belt buckle until his dick is free. Rolling it in my palm, I scoot my knees down until I'm bending over him. My lips lower onto his cock, and he groans as I slide him into my mouth.

"Oh, baby girl, you don't have to do that."

I pop him out of my mouth just long enough to answer. "But I like it."

My tongue flicks over his rim as my hands tug at his shaft.

"How did I get so lucky?" he groans as he lies back on the bed.

The groans tell me that he likes it, and I lose myself in pleasuring him. Sucking and nibbling and licking until I'm so wet I can hardly stand it.

My hand slides into my panties, and I circle my clit as I take long sucks of his cock.

"God, you're incredible," he moans, his gaze meeting mine.

I suck so hard my cheeks pull inwards.

"I'm close, baby girl."

My hand slides to his balls, and I rub them as I suck his juicy cock. My pleasure builds, and as he explodes in my mouth, my body shatters into a million pieces in a spine-tingling orgasm.

Hot cum hits the back of my throat, and I swallow it down, not wasting a drop.

When my body stops trembling, he pulls me up to lie next to him on the bed.

"That was incredible. You're incredible."

"Thanks."

I snuggle into his arms, feeling smug that I can give this man so much pleasure. His arm goes around me, pulling me tightly into his side.

But as we lay there, tucked in together, I wonder what happens when this is all over. Because it's not just that I don't want to go back to my old life. I don't want to go back to a life without Will.

15

WILL

*L*ater that afternoon, we're driving down the highway to the Underground Crows' HQ. I'm not sure if it's a bad idea taking Chastity with me, but I can't refuse her anything when she's got her plump hand on my cock.

Besides, if she stays in the car, I don't see how it can hurt.

I glance over at Chastity as we drive. She's got the window down with one hand sticking out of it. She's got her eyes closed, feeling the breeze against her skin.

She looks beautiful—hell, she always looks beautiful. But never so much as when she doesn't know I'm watching her.

The last three weeks have been the happiest of my life. Hanging out with Chastity, breaking into houses, and the hot sex that comes after.

But there's still so much she's holding back, I'm sure of it.

I've heard her on the phone having heated conversations, but all she says afterwards is that she was talking to her mom. She brushes me off when I ask about her family. I guess she wants to get away from them, and I'm happy to oblige.

When I started planning my sailing trip, it was just going to be me. But now I can't imagine leaving Chastity behind. I haven't asked her yet, but tonight I'm going to ask if she wants to come with me.

I can imagine us sailing down the coast of Peru, stopping in at small seaside towns, eating seafood by the water, doing a few hits of rich tourists, then moving on to the next place.

With Chastity by my side, the trip takes on a whole new adventure, and I hope like hell she wants to come with me.

We pull into the parking lot of the Underground Crows, and Chastity puts her hands to her mouth.

"This is who you sell the jewelry to?"

I can't tell if she's impressed or disgusted. Not everyone agrees with what the Crows do, but I'm a thief. Who am I to judge?

"I have a buyer here. I don't ask what they do with it. I just take the cash and go."

She's sitting upright, her gaze taking in the bikes and the outside of the bar. She looks impressed.

"You stay put in the car. I'll be about twenty minutes."

"Okay."

"Then I'm taking you out for a crayfish lunch."

I give her a kiss on the lips before getting out of the car.

Gage is at the bar when I walk in, and he nods at me. "I'll be with you in a minute."

While I wait for Gage, I head to the bar, and one of the bartenders hands me a beer. I'm sipping it slowly when a ripple of chatter goes around the room. All eyes turn to stare at the door, and I follow their gaze.

Chastity is standing in the doorway looking uncertain. I'm annoyed she's in here, and I'm especially not crazy about all these men looking at her. Abandoning my beer, I quickly go to her.

When her eyes find mine, she looks relieved. "Sorry, Will. I need the toilet."

The annoyance melts out of me. I can never stay angry at Chastity for long. "It's okay, babe."

But I wonder if it's just an excuse to see the inside of the club, something else that's new and different from the life she's used to.

A hand comes down on my shoulder, and I turn to see Gage.

His eyes rake up and down Chastity in a way that makes me uneasy. I take her hand protectively. "She's with me."

His eyebrows shoot up into his head, and his gaze transfers from Chastity to me. "Is she now?"

There's something off about his tone, but before I can call him out on it, Chastity speaks up.

"Could I please borrow your bathroom?"

Gage looks amused and signals to the woman behind the bar. "Gina, take this little lady to the restroom."

Gina smiles kindly and indicates for Chastity to follow her.

"When she's done, give her a drink and keep her company while I talk to Will upstairs."

Gina nods, and I hear what he's really asking. Keep an eye on her, and don't let her go wondering around.

I follow Gage upstairs and to the room where we do business.

"Sorry, man. She was meant to wait in the car."

Gage holds up a hand to cut me off. "I didn't know you were running 'round with Chastity Fletcher."

My breath catches. How does Gage know her name? And why is that surname familiar? That's not the surname Chastity gave me.

"Who?"

Gage shakes his head slowly. "Come on, man. You mean to tell me you don't know who she is?"

My stomach clenches. I feel like I'm on the edge of a precipice and everything I know about Chastity is about the collapse in around me.

I know she likes to sing in the shower. I know she has a birth-mark on her left shoulder that looks like a strawberry. And I know the sounds she makes when I make her come with my tongue. But do I really know who Chastity is?

Then it hits me why the name is so familiar. "You mean from Fletcher's Holdings?"

They own half the Sunset Coast. They buy and sell commercial real estate for maximum profit, not caring whose livelihoods are affected along the way. It was the closing of Fletcher-owned warehouses that left the residents of Temptation Bay without jobs or prospects.

And it's run by a property mogul who isn't afraid to be on the wrong side of the law to get what he wants. "She's Damon Fletcher's daughter?"

Gage nods, and I fall over the precipice. For a moment, I can't breathe. The room's too hot, and I pull at my collar.

Everything Chastity told me about herself is a lie.

"She's his daughter." I have to say it again because I still can't believe it. I push the chair back and pace the room.

"You didn't know?"

"Nope."

"Ah, shit. Sorry, man. Both of his daughters have gone missing, and the man is pissed off."

"She's not missing. She's with me."

Gage gives me a pointed look. "And if he finds her with you, you're a dead man."

"But she's been talking to her family…" I trail off, suddenly not so sure. She told me her family knows she's safe, but maybe she hasn't spoken to them at all. "Shit."

Gage shakes his head. "Looks like she really did a number on you."

That's an understatement. It feels like my insides are falling out and my heart's shattered into pieces. Everything I thought we had is based on a lie. I don't know who Chastity is at all.

"Sorry, man, but let's do business. Then you can sort out the shit with your woman."

In a daze, I take the velvet roll out of my pocket and lay down the goods. But the entire time, I'm pacing, wondering how I could have been so stupid to let a privileged, poor little rich girl get one over on me.

CHASTITY

Gina makes me a vodka and coke, and we chat while I wait for Will. I've never been in an MC clubhouse before, and it's cozier than I imagined.

A group of men sits around a table, their heads bent together in quiet discussion, and another woman stops by the bar to chat with Gina.

It feels like a family to me, more so than mine ever has.

There's movement on the stairs, and I turn to find Will storming down them. His expression is dark, and he doesn't look at me.

A shiver runs down my spine. Something's up. He wouldn't be that mad at me just for following him in. Maybe the deal didn't go well.

I say a quick goodbye to Gina and meet Will at the bottom of the stairs.

"Let's go." He doesn't look at me when he says it and strides ahead of me to the car.

A feeling of trepidation grows in my stomach. "Did everything go okay?"

He doesn't reply, but once in the car, he pulls out an envelope full of money. He splits it in half and shoves the wad of cash at me.

"Here's your half."

I've never thought that half of the earnings would be mine. I was only ever doing this for the thrill. It's not like I need money.

"Keep it. Put it toward your boat."

He shakes but won't look at me. "I don't want it."

He shoves the money at me, and it lands in my lap.

"Will?" His expression is fierce, his tone cold like nothing I've ever heard from him. "What is it?"

Will starts the car and keeps his eyes straight ahead on the road.

"Why didn't you tell me you were Damon Fletcher's daughter."

Ah, shit. My heart misses a beat, and the ball in my gut tightens. I don't know what to say. I've been found out, and I don't have a good reason.

"Well?" he demands, glancing at me as he drives. "Why did you lie to me?"

"I didn't mean to."

My voice is a whisper, and I hate how weak I sound. But I hate Will being angry with me and what this could mean.

"I didn't think you'd want me if you knew who I was."

"You can say that again. Do you know what your father is?"

There it is. The shadow of my family that I must always walk under. "Yes. Yes, I do."

"He's a ruthless bastard who doesn't care about anyone."

I flinch at the words even though I know they're true. Dad has stepped on a lot of people to build his empire without caring how he had to do it.

"I know. That's why I don't want to go back."

It's as if he hasn't heard me—or doesn't want to.

"That night I met you. You said you were looking for a friend. What were you really doing?"

I hang my head. He's catching me in every single lie I told him, and I want the earth to open up and swallow me.

"It's true that I dropped out of college. But I wasn't looking for my friend." I give a big sigh, knowing that he'll hate me when I come clean.

"I was outside that house because that's my parents' house."

"You saw me steal from your family and you let me do it?"

The look on his face is part incredulous and part disgusted, and it makes me flinch. I guess he's got the wrong impression about happy families. "You don't know my family."

"I know enough."

"Not all families are happy, Will. My father's a ruthless asshole who cares more about making money than his own family. And my mother's too concerned about keeping up appearances to notice that her own daughters are desperately unhappy."

"No wonder you both ran away."

It takes me a moment to understand what he just said. "Trinity ran away?"

He throws a glance at me, and for a moment, I see a flash of concern until he rearranges his features into something harder.

"Yeah, your 'friend' Trinity."

I remember the half-truth I told Will. That Trinity was a friend, and I'd spent the happiest times of my life with her in Cod Cove. The last part wasn't a lie. My sister and I had a wonderful childhood playing on the beach while our parents were too busy sucking up to the locals to worry about what we were doing.

If Trinity's run away and my parents don't know where I am, mom will be distraught. She may not win any mother-of-the-year awards, but she's still my mom.

"I want to go home."

My voice comes out small. But suddenly, I don't want to be with Will. I lied to him, and he clearly hates me. I want to get as far away from him as possible, where I can't hurt him anymore.

"Good 'cause that's exactly where I'm taking you."

The rest of the drive is silent. He's so angry I know there's no point in trying to talk to him. Besides, what else is there to say?

I'm the antithesis of what he stands for. My family rides roughshod over the poor, doing whatever they can to make their fortune, while Will picks up the pieces, delivering food to those in need. There's no way we can be together, no way we ever should have even met.

We turn into Cod Cove, and he pulls over near the beach. Before I get out of the car, I turn to Will. He keeps his eyes ahead, refusing to look at me.

"I'm so sorry I lied to you, Will. But these have been the best weeks of my life. You made me forget I was a Fletcher. For a few weeks, I was someone else. I was someone better."

I slam the door shut, and as Will drives off, I let the tears stream down my cheeks.

17

WILL

The slamming of the car door reverberates through my head, and I seal my heart shut with it.

I can't get out of Cod Cove quick enough. I don't look back as I drive up the windy road, leaving Chastity-fucking-Fletcher where she belongs.

But she belongs with you. My heart whispers.

I clench my chest tight, trying to push the ache out of my heart.

I thought she was something special. I thought we had something special. But she's just a rich kid looking for a bit of excitement. There's no way she could have coped slumming it on a measly thirty-foot yacht.

A wave of nausea goes through me. Chastity must have thought I was ridiculous with my pathetic dream when her family probably owns a small armada of super-yachts.

My hands grip the steering wheel until my knuckles turn white as I try to banish all thoughts of Chastity from my mind.

I'm still in a foul mood as I pull up to the marina a half hour later.

"How's it going, Will?" Freddy's grin slides of his face when he sees my expression.

I pull out the wad of cash from my envelope and slam it on the desk in front of him. "Got the last payment for you, Freddy."

He takes the bills. I can tell he wants to ask me where the money came from, all piled up neatly in a white envelope. But Freddy's smarter than that.

He counts out the money and hands me back a stack of bills. "I better get you the key."

Freddy's grinning as he hands over the key to the yacht. I should be too. I've been working up to this moment for months. But all I feel is empty.

Key in hand, I go to take a look at her, making a list of what I need to get her into shape.

It's not too bad. Some minor repairs, a good scrub down, a few licks of paint and she'll be seaworthy.

When I step back onto the jetty, Freddy's scrubbing it down. He looks up at me with that easy grin of his.

"When you leaving on the big trip?"

"As soon as possible."

"That lovely young lady going with you?"

At the mention of Chastity, my chest tightens. "No."

I turn away quickly and stride down the pier so Freddy can't see my heart breaking.

18

CHASTITY

There's a tentative knock on the door, and Mom slides a carefully manicured hand around the doorframe. "Can I come in?"

I don't bother looking up, not wanting to see the disappointment in her eyes. "Whatever."

She takes that to mean yes and pushes open the door. Her gaze sweeps the room, taking in the clothes strewn on the floor and dirty plates on the dresser.

I'm lying on the bed, and she sits next to me, her hand tucking a strand of hair behind my ear. "You need to wash your hair, honey."

I can feel her eyes raking over me, taking in my ice-cream-stained sweatpants that I've worn for the last three days, ever since I came back home.

"I'll run you a bath. You can use my tub."

"No thanks."

"I'll add bubbles. I've got this divine bubble bath from the salon. It's peony and peppercorns."

My face screws up at the sound of that. But I can tell she's

68

trying to be nice. Despite all my mom's flaws, she does seem genuinely concerned about me.

"You need to have a wash, sweetie, and get yourself cleaned up."

"What's the point?" *If Will can't see me*, I want to add.

It's as if she reads my thoughts. "I don't get dressed up every day to look good for your father. I dress up every day to look good for *me*."

She emphasizes the word "me."

"What I'm saying, sweetie, is whoever he is, there's no excuse for unwashed hair. Don't give him that power."

A chuckle escapes my lips. Letting your hair go greasy is a big sin in my mom's eyes.

I turn my head to face her, and she smiles down at me. A tired, worn smile. She's looking older all of a sudden. The lines around her mouth are visible, and there are dark circles under her eyes.

Mom's got a lot to worry about at the moment, and I'm adding to that by moping around. "Okay, okay. You can run me a bath."

Her smile softens, and some of the concern slides off her face.

"But there better be a tub of ice cream and a big spoon on the side."

"I prefer a glass of champagne, but if that's what you need, honey…"

"Yes, it is what I need."

Mom gets up off the bed and crosses to the door.

My parents were surprisingly calm when I wandered into the house three days ago. I had told mom I was staying with a friend so she wasn't completely worried about me, but Trinity has disappeared without a trace, only leaving a note saying not to try to find her.

It seems her running away has overshadowed any trouble I might have been in.

"Mom." She turns at the door. "Does it ever bother you? What dad does?"

I don't know all of my father's dealings, but I know it's not all legitimate. He has a lot of people he calls "business associates" who seem like thugs to me. I know he's not well liked in the community, but as I've gotten older, I've started to wonder exactly what it is he's into.

"It's complicated," Mom sighs and leans against the door-frame. "Your father owned only one warehouse when I met him. He was excited. He had plans. I knew it wasn't all, um..." She searches around for the words. We've never spoken this candidly before, and I hold my breath, wanting her to go on. "...on the right side of the law."

She looks me in the eye as she says it, and I feel an understanding pass between us, that she's talking to me as an adult, letting me into the harsh reality of the way the world works.

"But he was so charismatic," she continues, "and it was so much more exciting than the farm I grew up on in Kentucky."

There's a light in her eyes as she reminisces about her early days with dad, and it reminds me of the last few weeks I've spent with Will.

Maybe mom was the same. Maybe she got sucked in by a charismatic thief, and before she knew it, she was married to a property mogul who isn't afraid to do anything it takes to get what he wants.

"If I met your father now," she says slowly, "I'm not sure I'd feel the same. But once you two girls came along, we were bound together. There was no way to get out, even if I wanted to."

She's looking somewhere out the window, and a slight smile appears on her face.

"But I don't want to. Your father may be a hard man to some, but he's always been good to me. He's never strayed, he's always looked after me, and he's always buying me trinkets."

She breaks out of her reverie.

"Oh, that reminds me. We dismissed the cleaner. Turns out she was stealing my jewelry."

There's a lump in my throat, and I swallow it down.

Mom waves her hand dismissively. "She only took a few items. Some earrings and a gold bracelet. Left your grandmother's ring, thankfully."

I don't hear the rest of what she's saying. I'm thinking of Will, of what he thought was a victimless crime. But a woman has lost her job because of him, falsely accused and sent away with no references.

Mom's right. It might start with petty crimes, but it will never be enough. Before long, he'll be doing whatever it takes to protect his interests.

Will may think he's different, but in reality, he'll end up exactly like my father.

19

WILL

Rain pounds relentlessly into the dirt paths of the trailer park, turning potholes into puddles.

It's rained endlessly for the last two days, meaning I haven't been able to work on the boat. The boat is the only thing that's kept me from going insane in the week since Chastity exited my life.

But since it's been raining, I've been stuck inside. Alone. Remembering every time we made love, every time we laughed together, every time my heart opened up to Chastity a little bit more.

Jumping around a muddy bit of path, my foot slips and comes down directly into a cold puddle, instantly soaking my foot.

"Shit."

My boots are soaked by the time I get to the last trailer in the park and drop the plastic bag on the wooden step that leads to Sue's front door.

There's a plastic awning around the entrance to her trailer, and the rain runs off it in heavy rivulets.

As I place the bag in the sheltered area, the door flies open. "For God's sake, Will, get out of the rain."

Sue pulls me inside, crossly taking in my soaked clothes and dripping hair.

"What you doing running 'round in the rain for?"

She fusses over me like my mother would if she were still alive. And I let her, easing out of my dripping coat and accepting the offered towel to dry my hair off.

It's cold in the trailer, and it's only now that there's a guest does Sue flick on the small wall heater. She must sit in the cold on her own to save a few dollars.

While Sue's busy filling the kettle, I slip a hundred-dollar bill under a vase. It'll be enough to keep the heat on for a few months.

I dry off while she makes the coffee. Then we sit at her little table with the sound of the rain hitting the tin roof above us.

"You're not going to see me for a while, Sue."

Her face looks grim, but she nods. "You finally got your boat ready?"

"Almost. I'll be heading off once I get the final coat of paint done."

She looks out at the rain streaking down the window. "You've been good to us, Will. I'm glad you're finally getting to live your dream and get the hell out of here."

The old lady smiles wistfully. She's genuinely happy for me. Happier than I feel.

"I need your help, Sue."

Her hand goes over mine in a motherly way. "Tell me what you need, dear."

"I've worked things out with Freddy. I'll be putting money in his account each month, but he doesn't know what everyone here needs."

Sue rolls her eyes. "Course he doesn't. That man never knew what was good for anyone."

I let the comment slide. There's some history between Freddy and Sue, although I've never been sure what it is.

"You'll need to see him every week. Tell him who's in the most need. What size diapers or which baby formula to buy."

Sue sighs. "If I must see that man every week, then I will." As she says it, her hand comes up to push her hair up, and I get the impression she won't mind seeing Freddy every week at all.

"Good. I'm counting on the both of you."

Sue sits up straighter. "I'll keep my end of the bargain. You can count on me, Will." Her eyes narrow. "But how will you afford it?"

"Don't you worry about me. I always know how to get a bit of extra cash."

A flicker of suspicion crosses her face.

Sue's never known how I make my money. She was a good friend of my mother's, and it would break her heart if she knew what I had gotten into. I give her my most winning smile.

"Everyone always needs a handyman."

Her eyes soften. "Good because with the two of you now…"

I look away. "There's not two of us, only me."

"What happened to Chastity?"

The mention of her name makes my chest tighten. I have to look away so Sue doesn't see my expression, but nothing gets passed her keen eyes. "You didn't let her get away, did you?"

More like I dropped her off and told her she wasn't welcome in my life. The fact I've broken my own heart makes it that much worse.

"It's not that simple."

Her hand squeezes mine. "It never is, dear."

Which is probably true, but how can I forgive someone who lied to me?

"Do you know she's the daughter of Damon Fletcher?"

Sue's brow furrows. "The guy from Fletcher's Holdings?"

"Yeah. The guy who closed his warehouses, sold off his land to developers, and left everyone here out of a job."

Sue tuts, shaking her head in disapproval. "Not a popular family around Temptation Bay."

"That's an understatement."

"The person who moves business forward is never popular. It's a hard pill to swallow, but I'm sure there was a reason for shutting down the warehouses here."

"Yeah, so he could use cheap labor across the border."

Sue shrugs. "It did make room for that new shopping development that they're planning."

I stare at Sue. She lost her job and was thrown into poverty. How can she be so positive? "You gonna get a job there?"

"I doubt they want a woman pushing sixty. But half the men here have signed up to work on the construction site. There will be jobs coming here, Will. Things don't stay down forever."

It's a new perspective for me. The last few years have been hard on this community, yet Sue is more positive than I am.

She points a bony finger at me. "The sins of the father are not visited on the daughter. Especially when she's a lovely girl like Chastity."

I stare at her. "You know who Chastity is and you don't mind?"

Sue shrugs. "There's too much hate in this world, Will. Why not show a little forgiveness?"

My hand goes to my chin, and I rub it absentmindedly. My stubble's longer than usual, and I realize I can't remember the last time I shaved.

"What I'm saying, dear, is you can't blame Chastity for what her family is. If you love her, what does it matter?"

"It matters to me. Her father doesn't play by the book, and it's not right."

Sue takes a sip of coffee, eyeing me over her mug. "Do you always play by the book, Will?"

She gives me a pointed look, and I can't meet her eye. Damn, she does know what I do, or at least has her suspicions.

But she's right. Who am I to judge?

I tell myself I don't hurt other people, that stealing jewelry off the rich is a victimless crime. But I'm still a criminal. Maybe I'm no better than Chastity's father.

"All I'm saying, dear, is if I had someone who looked at me the way that girl looks at you, I'd grab them with both hands and never let them go."

Her words strike at something deep inside me. The constriction in my chests lessens a little. Could it be that Chastity loves me? Am I being foolish to care so much about what her family is?

I've been a fool. It doesn't matter who she is. I know that I love her. I love her so deeply that I can't be without her.

I stand up suddenly, making the trailer shake. "I gotta go, Sue."

It's still raining outside, but she doesn't try to stop me. There's a twinkle in her eye that makes her look younger and livelier as she waves me off. "You go get her, Will."

2 0

CHASTITY

he hairbrush catches on my wet tresses, and I tug at it roughly, not caring about the hair that comes out on the brush or the sting of my scalp.

I've been going through the motions for my mother's sake, having a bath and washing my hair. But there's still a blackness that envelopes my heart, and it feels like I'll never be free of it.

Giving up on my hair, I plonk my brush down on the dresser.

There's a sound at the window, and I cross the room to investigate. The rain that fell all day has stopped, but maybe it dislodged something in the guttering.

The curtain billows open, and I freeze. There's no way I had that window open today. I'm transfixed as a hand pulls back the curtain.

Someone tumbles through the window, falling hard on the floor and pulling one side of the curtain off its hooks.

"Shit." The figure rolls onto the ground and sits up.

"Will?"

My heart leaps in my throat, and I can't breathe. He gets to his feet, rubbing his knee.

"That's not an easy climb, getting up to your window."

It's so good to see him and a relief to hear his voice. The last time we spoke, he was cold, unfeeling. Now as he rubs his knee, he seems to be his usual self.

"What are you doing here?"

He cocks his head sideways. "I miss you, Chastity. I'm miserable without you. I came to get you."

It's everything I've been hoping he'd say. The blackness around my heart parts a little bit, and I dare to feel something I haven't all week. Hope.

But something's bothering me. I fold my arms in front of my body, putting a barrier between us.

"You dropped me off back here, Will. Discarded me like I meant nothing. That hurt."

He winces, and a flicker of pain crosses his face. "I'm sorry, Chastity. I was so angry that you lied to me. I felt foolish, like you'd taken me for a ride, slumming it with the poor kid for a thrill."

I hang my head, my arms falling to my sides. "It wasn't like that. I'm sorry I lied. I knew you wouldn't want anything to do with me if you knew who I was."

"You were right."

My chest tightens, and the blackness closes back over my heart. Did he come all this way to reject me again?

Will takes two steps across the room until he's facing me.

"But I didn't realize that I couldn't live without you, that my life is meaningless unless you're in it."

He cups my chin in his hand and lifts my face until I'm looking into his dark eyes. "I love you, Chastity. I don't care who you are or what your family has done. I love you Chastity."

The blackness melts away from my heart, and I blink back tears at the love I see reflected in his expression.

"I've been miserable without you, Will."

His fingers graze my cheek, making me shudder at my need for his touch. "You'll never be without me again, babygirl."

"But I'll always be in the shadow of my family, you have to understand that."

"Not if we get away from here. Come with me on my yacht. Sail away with me."

My mind's racing, and a sweet buzz spreads through my body. There's a tug of excitement in my core, and I know this is what I want to do. To go on an adventure with Will.

"Okay."

As the smile spreads across my face, he captures my lips in a kiss. I press against him, savoring the taste of him that I've been missing.

Too soon, he breaks away. "Pack your bags, babygirl, and let's get out of here."

He moves to the window, but I shake my head. "I'm not sneaking out. This time, we're going out the front door."

It's important to me that my family accepts my choice. No more sneaking around. I need to show them I make my own decisions now. Besides, if we sneak off again, dad will send his henchmen looking for us.

Will nods, seeming to understand. "If that's what you want to do."

I pack a small bag, just the essentials. There's not much room on a boat. Will waits by the door, and when I'm ready, he takes my hand.

"You ready?" I nod, and he opens the door.

Clutching Will's hand, I lead him downstairs. My parents are in the living room, and my dad barely looks up from his paperwork when I walk in. But when he sees Will, he sets his glasses down slowly.

"Who's this, and what's he doing in my house?"

"I'm Will Baker, and I'm taking your daughter."

My chest swells with pride at the way Will stands up to my dad.

Dad stands up slowly. He's an imposing man at his full height, and I'm sure he uses that to intimidate people, but Will doesn't back down.

"My daughter isn't going anywhere with you."

I can feel the rage bubbling inside me. I'm tired of other people deciding my life.

"I am," I blurt out. "We're going on Will's yacht as far away from here as possible."

Will squeezes my hand, and it gives me the strength not to flinch when my dad turns his penetrating gaze on me.

"Don't be ridiculous." Dad waves his hand dismissively at me, as if what I want doesn't matter. "You're staying right here and going back to finish your degree."

"I don't want to—"

Dad cuts me off. "And when we do find you a suitable partner, it won't be some small-time petty thief."

Will freezes beside me, and my dad gives him a satisfied look.

"That's right. Don't think I don't know who you are. Not much happens up this coast that I don't know about."

"I'm going legitimate. I'll be chartering the yacht for paying customers."

Dad smirks. "I don't care that you're a thief. Christ, it shows you've got a bit of backbone. But my daughter deserves more than the likes of you can offer her."

"No."

We all turn to stare at my mother's interruption. She's been standing quietly in the corner, her lips pulled into a thin line, her knuckles white.

She swallows hard, and her lips turn up in a smile, which she fixes on dad. "I mean, don't you think, dear, it's time we let Chastity make some choices herself?"

Sidling over to her husband, she rubs a hand over his back. Dad closes his eyes and leans into her touch.

"Look where that's gotten her. She's a dropout running around with a thief." They're talking about me like I'm not here. But I've never seen this side of my mom, the way she's manipulating my dad like he's a piece of putty.

"Or," she says, running her hands over his shoulder, "she's a young woman who's found love and has an exciting adventure ahead of her. It reminds me of when we first met, dear."

She whispers the last part in his ear, a warm smile on her face. For a moment, I can see the young woman she once was, laughing and carefree, setting off on a life of adventure with the man she loves.

Dad gives her a warm look and takes her hands in his.

"We've driven both our daughters away, Damon. We may never find Trinity, but I can't bear to lose Chastity as well."

It's a rare moment of love between my parents, and I can't help staring. But this decision isn't up to them.

"We're going whether I have your blessing or not." I stand up taller and Will squeezes my hand. "I don't know what the future holds for us, but this is my choice. And I choose Will."

Dad rubs his eyes, suddenly looking tired. "Fine. You have my blessing. On one condition." The soft expression falls from his face, and he gives me a hard look.

"You keep in touch with your mother. Wherever you sail off to. She needs phone calls, postcards… And if you hear anything about your sister, you tell us straight away."

"I will."

Mom opens her arms and enfolds me in a hug. There are tears running down her perfectly made-up face. "I didn't realize how precious my daughters were to me until I lost you both."

I wrap my arms around her and we embrace like we haven't done for years. "You haven't lost me, Mom."

Pulling away from my parents, I find Will waiting for me. He holds out a hand. "You ready?"

I swipe at the tears on my face. How is it possible to be so excited about something but feel sad at the same time?

I slip my hand into Will's, and the heat from him—the raw energy—courses through my body. "I'm ready."

EPILOGUE ONE

CHASTITY

Two weeks later…

A strip of light peeks in from the bottom of the blindfold, and I squeeze my eyes shut. I want my first look at the yacht to be as much of a surprise as Will does.

He hasn't let me near it for the last two weeks as he put the finishing touches on her. He didn't want me to see it again until he'd done the refurb.

But that's fine by me. I've spent the last two weeks buying supplies, plotting a course, and brushing up on my Spanish.

Will stops in front of me, and I collide into him. I let my body rest against his back, enjoying the solid feeling of him.

"Are you ready to see your new home?"

"Yes," I squeal impatiently.

Will undoes the blindfold and slowly lowers it from my eyes.

The sight in front of me is beyond anything I expected. When he first showed me the run-down thirty-foot yacht, I wasn't sure it was seaworthy.

But now, the decks have been sanded, polished, and painted.

There are plump cream cushions on the seating, and the railings are polished to a shiny sheen.

"Well?"

Will sounds nervous, and I realize I haven't spoken yet. "She's beautiful."

"Yup." He runs a hand over the railing. "She is."

My eyes notice the writing on the side, and I gasp. In flowing script, freshly painted is the word "Chastity."

"You renamed her?"

Will's smiling. "After the second most important girl in my life."

I push him playfully. "What do I have to do to get ahead of the boat on that list?"

His eyes glint wickedly, and he stoops quickly, his hand going under my knees to scoop me into his arms. "I can think of something."

Will carries me onto the boat and sets me down on the deck. I run my hands along the polished railing, excitement tingling through my body. This is our home. This is where the adventure begins.

"Show me below deck."

It's even more impressive below. Will has kept the dark wood from the eighties but modernized the functionality. There's a modern stove along with a comfortable-looking sofa and table.

A set of stairs leads to a master bedroom. This is where I go, Will trailing behind.

The boat rocks gently, and the sound of the water hitting the gunwale is peaceful. We're pointing out of the jetty, and the only thing beyond the windows is open ocean.

"It's beautiful, Will." His arms slide around my waist, and I lean my back into him.

"You're beautiful." His mouth kisses my neck, and a delicious shiver runs down my body.

I reach my arm up around his neck as he plants kisses behind my ear. My body tingles as his hand slides over my belly and down between my legs. "How about we christen her?"

It's the middle of the afternoon and there's people on the jetty, but the tug low in my belly is too strong to ignore. "Sounds like a good idea."

I press my backside into him, feeling his hardness pressing back.

His hands bunch up my skirt, and his fingers brush against my thigh. I shiver at the touch, willing him to move his hand higher.

His fingers brush my panties, and I let out a moan. "You're already wet."

There's a hint of excitement in his voice, and his mouth crashes down on my neck, racing over my throat as one hand slides over my wet panties, the other over my breasts.

I push my hips back, grinding into him until I'm leaning forward, almost bent double.

My skirt flicks right up, and he yanks at my panties, pulling them down my legs and off my feet. I shiver as the sea air hits my bare skin. At the same time, his finger runs over my slit, making all my nerve endings tingle.

A moan escapes my lips, and I press my hips back, unashamed to show my neediness.

"Oh, babygirl. You're so sexy." As he says it, I feel the bare skin of his dick brush against my opening.

"Will." My voice is pleading. "I want you."

He gives a low chuckle. "I can tell, babygirl."

The hard tip of his cock slides between my folds, hovering just inside my entrance. My heart's hammering in my chest. We've always been so careful with using protection, and this is the first time I've felt him bare-skinned and inside me.

I run through all of the possible scenarios in my head. I'm with the man I love. I don't care if I get pregnant.

Giving him no time to think, I push my hips back, sliding

myself down his bare cock. The sensation makes me gasp, and Will lets out a groan.

"Chastity…" I wiggle my hips, and whatever he was going to say turns into a groan. "Fuuuck."

I push myself back and forth on him, loving the fact that despite being bent over across the bed, I'm the one holding the power."Touch my breasts, Will."

His hands move obligingly over my breasts, pulling my dress and bra down until he finds my nipples. His fingers pull at the hard nubs, sending shock waves coursing through my body and down to my core.

With one hand, he's strumming my nipple. With the other, he's holding my hips, pulling me onto himself.

His cock knocks on the front wall of my womb, going deeper than he's ever been and causing a delicious pressure to build there.

"Fuck, Will!" I cry out, and he thrusts deeper, until my body is pulled tight and there's nothing it can do but explode. I come hard, crying out his name as his cock slams into me.

I feel Will tense, then the sweet sensation of his seed coating my walls in long, wet ropes. His body jams against mine, fitting neatly against me.

He leans forward and kisses my neck, softly this time. "That was amazing. You're amazing."

Will slides out of me, and we fall exhausted onto the bed. "I think I need an afternoon nap."

He pulls me toward him and we lie together, listening to the sound of the water lapping against the side of the boat.

I run my finger over his arm, thinking about our new home, our adventure.

Will's promised to go legit, so we'll be earning money the honest way, picking up odd jobs where we can and taking out tourists for day trips on the yacht.

We won't have any luxuries, but I don't mind. As long as I have Will, that's all I need.

EPILOGUE TWO

WILL

Six years later…

My eyes scan the jetty and come to rest on Freddy holding a clipboard and directing a man who's pushing a cart full of luggage.

Freddy smiles when he sees me strolling over. "Everything okay, boss?"

I've told him a hundred times not to call me that. But he always does it with a toothless grin that I find endearing.

"You seen my wife anywhere?"

He points to the reception area of the William Baker Luxury Yacht Charters' office, where I can see two figures through the glass.

"Gossiping with my wife, as usual." He does a mock roll of the eyes, but I know he wouldn't have it any other way.

Strolling to the office, I push open the door just as Chastity throws her head back in a hearty laugh. Her hair falls loose over her shoulders, and the crinkle lines around her eyes give her a carefree look. I thought she was beautiful when I met her, but now, with six years of life experience etched into her face, she's stunning.

"What's the joke?"

Faking sternness, I look between Chastity and Sue, but they both keep their mouths firmly shut.

"Girl talk," says Sue with a wink at Chastity.

Employing Sue as my receptionist and booking coordinator was the best move for my business. She's coming up on retirement age, and I'm not sure how I'm going to replace her.

It didn't take her and Freddy long to rekindle their old flame, and we sailed back for the wedding a few years ago.

There's a pull on my leg, and I look down into the biggest, roundest blue eyes staring up at me. My daughter, Carley, smiles at me in a way I can never resist. "What is it, baby?"

I pick her up, and she leans her head against my shoulder, making my heart swell.

"I better get her down for a nap," says Chastity.

She rubs her belly, where our second baby is growing.

We spent an amazing few years traveling. Doing odd jobs where we could, catching fresh fish for dinner, and living a simple life.

It was when Chastity became pregnant that we decided to come back. I opened the business and employed as many of the locals as I could.

With the babies coming, I had to move my family into a proper home, but we still take to the ocean every chance we get.

"Put her on the couch here if you like. I'll watch her."

Sue is an unofficial grandma, looking after the little one as if she was her own.

"Are you sure?" Chastity asks.

"Of course," says Sue. "We've got our customers in for the day. I don't expect to be interrupted."

"Good." I slide my arm around Chastity's waist. "Because I'd like to take my wife out to lunch."

"Not for seafood," she says wistfully.

"Sorry, babygirl. No seafood for you." I rub her belly, and even that close contact has my dick twitching. I know what I'd like to give her for lunch, and if we're quick, we might just have time.

I hand Carley over to Sue. "Be good for Nana, okay?"

She nods her head solemnly, making her curly mop of hair bounce. Clasping Chastity's hand, I lead her outside.

"Where are we going?" she asks.

"Somewhere private."

Her head rests against my shoulder as we walk along the marina. My hand's in hers, and I run my thumb over the jewels on her fingers. They look good sparkling in the light against her sun-kissed skin.

I still have an eye for shiny things, but now I can afford to buy them for my wife. My thieving days are long gone, but the best thing I ever stole was Chastity's heart.

THE HENCHMAN'S OBSESSION

He'll risk everything for his one obsession...

Read Trinity and Karl's story in The Henchman's Obsession.

The moment I saw Trinity's photograph, my life changed.
Mine
Is all I can think as I track her down, scouring the country for my boss's daughter.
He thinks I'm bringing her home, but her home is with me now.
She wants a quiet life, I'll give it to her. I'll be the wholesome small-town man, if that's what she wants.
I'll be anything she needs me to be.
But she must never know that I work for her father...

mybook.to/TheHenchmansObsession

GET YOUR FREE BOOK

Sign up to the Sadie King mailing list for a FREE book!

You'll be the first to hear about new releases, exclusive offers, bonus content and all my news. You can even email me back. I love chatting with my readers!

To claim your free book visit:
www.authorsadieking.com/free

ABOUT THE AUTHOR

Sadie King is a USA Today Best Selling Author of short instalove romance.

She lives in New Zealand with her ex-military husband and raucous young son.

When she's not writing she loves catching waves with her son, running along the beach, and good wine, preferably drunk with a book in hand.

Keep in touch when you sign up for her newsletter. You'll even snag yourself a free short romance!

Visit: www.authorsadieking.com/free

www.authorsadieking.com